This Walker book belongs to:

_____

_____

For Fiona, story–spinner extraordinaire
MMc
For Papa Rudge and Mama Lou
LR

Published 2013 by Walker Books Ltd
87 Vauxhall Walk, London SE11 5HJ

10 9 8 7 6 5 4 3 2 1

Text © 2011 Meg McKinlay
Illustrations © 2011 Leila Rudge

This book has been typeset in Kosmik and Mrs Eaves

Printed in China

British Library Cataloguing in Publication Data:
a catalogue record for this book is available from the British Library

ISBN 978-1-4063-4930-6

www.walker.co.uk

NO BEARS

MEG McKINLAY

& LEILA RUDGE

WALKER BOOKS

AND SUBSIDIARIES

LONDON • BOSTON • SYDNEY • AUCKLAND

Hi! I'm Ruby and this is my book.

You can tell it's a book because there are words everywhere.

Words like

Once

upon

a

time

and *Happily ever after*

and
The
END.

I'm in charge of this book so I know everything about it –
including the most important thing, which is that there
are NO BEARS in it.

I'm tired of bears. Every time you read a book it's just
BEARS BEARS BEARS – horrible furry bears slurping
honey in grotty little caves.

You don't need BEARS for a book.

You need **pretty** things.

You need **fairies** and **princesses**

and **castles**.

You need **funny** things,

exciting things

and **scary** things.

Maybe a **monster**

or a **giant** or something.

Hmm, yes. I like the sound of that.

So, how about this?

Once upon a time

there was a beautiful princess.

The princess lived in a faraway castle with her father, the king, and her mother, the queen, and her fairy godmother, the fairy godmother.

But **NO BEARS**.

NOT

EVEN

ONE.

Yes, perfect! This is my kind of story. So ...

There were **NO BEARS** in the castle and there were **NO BEARS** in the village. There were **NO BEARS** in the whole entire kingdom or the next one or the next one.

There were **NO BEARS** in the deep dark forest in the faraway lands.

But what there **WAS** in the deep dark forest in the faraway lands was …

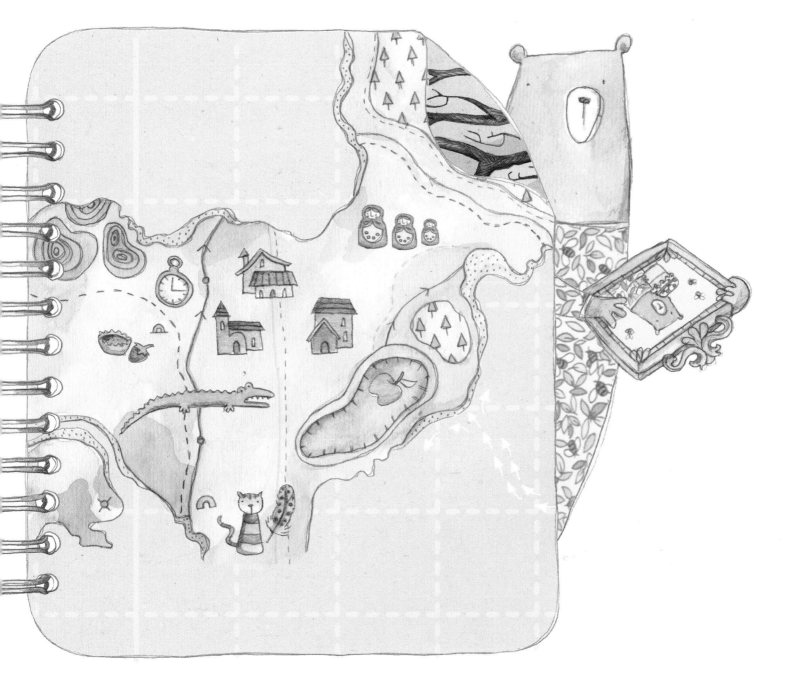

A MONSTER!

An evil, terrible monster who wanted to steal the princess away
so she could read him bedtime stories every night …

Ooh. This
is getting
scary.

One day, the monster set out from the faraway lands.

He climbed the mountain.

He crossed the river.

He stomped through the kingdom

and the next one

and the next one.

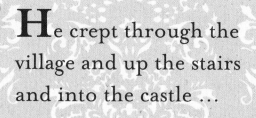

He crept through the village and up the stairs and into the castle ...

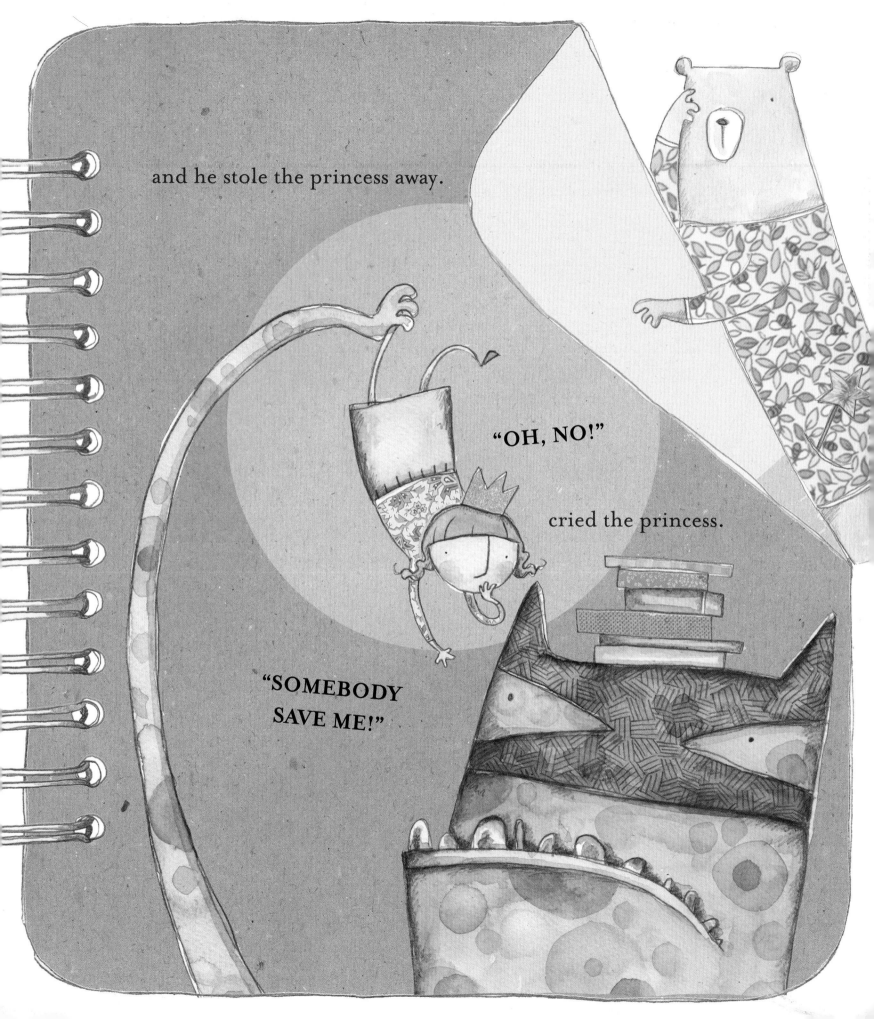

and he stole the princess away.

"OH, NO!"

cried the princess.

"SOMEBODY
SAVE ME!"

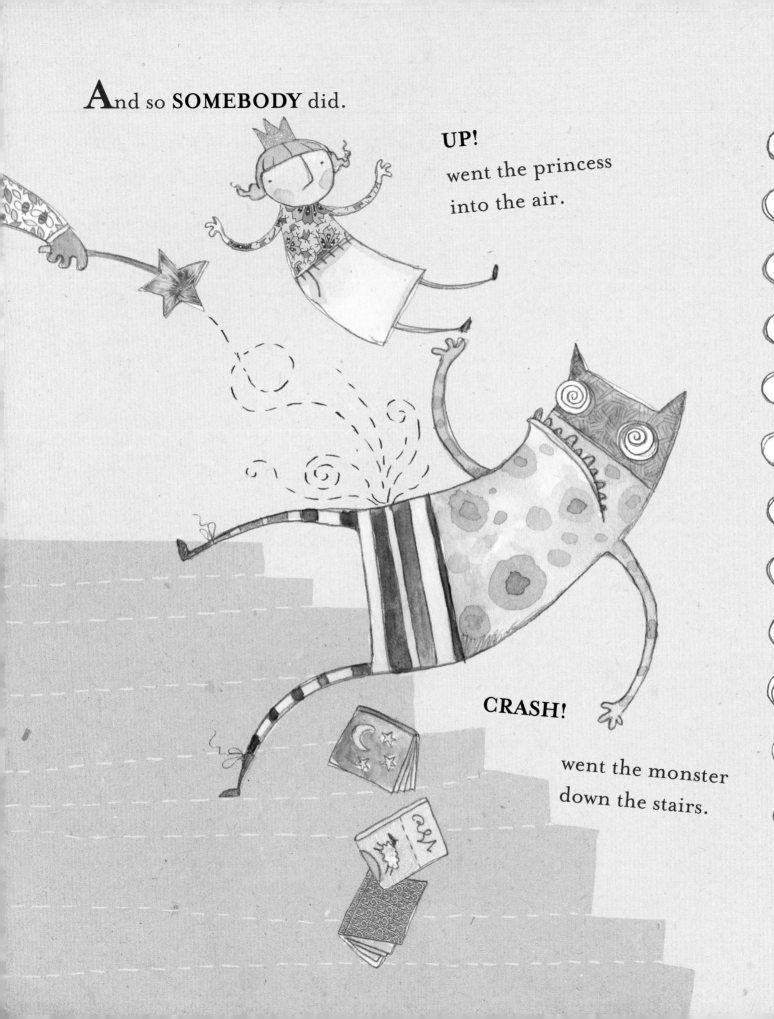

And so **SOMEBODY** did.

UP!

went the princess
into the air.

CRASH!

went the monster
down the stairs.

DOWN!

came the princess
safe in the tree.

SPLASH!

went the monster
into the sea.

Phew! That was close.

"Hooray!" cried the princess. "I'm saved."
Then her father, the king, and her mother,
the queen, threw a party for the fairy godmother.

Because everyone knew she was the one who had saved
the princess with her fantastical magic powers.

Wow! This has turned out to be a pretty good book, don't you think?

In fact, I think this has been the prettiest, most exciting, scariest and funniest book ever.

And I know why!

Because there are **NO BEARS** in it.

NOT ONE!

So now there's only one thing left to do.

And I think you know what that is.

It's to say that everyone lived

Happily ever after

in **The END.**

Meg McKinlay is a poet as well as a children's writer, whose previous titles include *The Truth About Penguins*. She divides her time between writing and teaching; she is an Honorary Research Associate at the University of Western Australia, where she has taught Australian literature, Japanese and creative writing. Meg lives with her family near the ocean in Fremantle, Western Australia.

Leila Rudge was born in England and grew up making mud pies with six siblings and Jeni from number 15. After completing an Illustration Degree at Bath Spa University, Leila headed to the southern hemisphere to seek her fortune (and the sunshine). Creating tiny characters for books is her favourite part of illustrating. Leila lives in Australia.

www.walker.co.uk